To Mare
Merry Christmas! loas of love
Mummy and Daddy
XXXX 25/12/01

THOMAS & FRIENDS
™

ANNUAL 2002

Illustrated by Robin Davies

Thomas the Tank Engine & Friends

A BRITT ALLCROFT COMPANY PRODUCTION

Based on The Railway Series by The Rev W Awdry

© Gullane (Thomas) LLC 2001

Published in Great Britain by Egmont World,
an imprint of Egmont Children's Books Limited,
239 Kensington High Street, London W8 6SA
Printed in Italy
ISBN 0 7498 5144 9

£5.99
UK only

Contents

Hello!

My name is Thomas the Tank Engine. I work on the railway with my engine friends. We work hard, but we have lots of fun and adventures, too. You can read all about them in the stories in this annual. There are puzzle pages and games to play, too. I hope you like them. Peep, peep!

From your friend

Thomas

A Special Day for Thomas

One day Thomas was talking to Duke, who is the oldest of the narrow-gauge engines. Duke was going off to do his favourite job, pulling the special picnic train full of summer visitors up to the lake. "It's a long, hard pull up the hills," Duke told Thomas. "But it's good fun, too. It's more like a day out than work."

"I wish I could have a day out," said Thomas. "I never go anywhere but my little Branch Line. It would be nice to see a bit of the world."

Duke smiled. "But your work is important, young Thomas," he said. "Just think what a mess your Branch Line would be in without you to run it! Why, everyone would be late, and Bertie the Bus would have a lot of extra work to do. And how would the men get to work at the quarry?"

"Yes, I know," said Thomas, but he couldn't help feeling just a little bit jealous of Duke.

Thomas was very busy for the rest of the day, but he didn't seem to be in his usual happy mood. He was a bit impatient with his coaches, Annie and Clarabel. "Come on, you two, get a move on!" he said to them. "I can't do all the work around here, you know. I'm never late, remember, not like some other engines I can think of. And I never take time off, not like Henry."

Annie and Clarabel tried to cheer Thomas up. They asked him to sing with them, which he usually likes doing. But Thomas wouldn't join in. "I'm much too busy for singing!" he said.

Thomas took some passengers to where Bertie the Bus was waiting to take them home. "I'm fed up of being stuck on this Branch Line," he said. "I never get a day off, you know."

By the time Thomas met James at the junction he was in an even worse mood. "What's wrong?" asked James, when he saw Thomas' miserable face.

"Duke has gone up to the lake with the picnic train," Thomas told James. "But I never go anywhere. I want a day out, too. It's just not fair!"

Thomas was grumpy. He usually peeped to say hello to the cows and sheep in the fields beside his line, but this time he ignored their friendly moos and baas.

When the fishermen fishing on the river bank waved to him as he went over the bridge, Thomas pretended he didn't see them.

9

At the end of the day Thomas took the men back home from work at the quarry. He heard one of the men talking to his Driver. "Don't forget that we won't be at work tomorrow," the man said. "The quarry is closing down for the day so we can all have a day out together at the beach."

Thomas felt sad. "Oh, no!" he said. "Everyone is having fun but me."

Thomas' Driver noticed that the little tank engine looked sad. "Is something wrong, Thomas?" he asked. "You're usually such a cheerful, happy little engine."

Thomas told him about Duke having a day out, and the men going to the beach. "I feel left out," said Thomas. "I want a special day, too."

Thomas' Driver smiled. "So that's it," he said. "But you're not being left out, Thomas. How do you think the men and their families are going to get to the beach tomorrow?"

"I don't know," said Thomas sadly. "Is Henry taking them? Or little Percy? Or is Bertie taking them by road?"

"No, they're going by train," said his Driver. "And a very special engine is going to pull the coaches. It's YOU, of course, Thomas. The men know how hard you work. They see you chuffing up and down your Branch Line every day. You're their favourite engine. They wouldn't let any other engine take them for their day out."

"ME?" said Thomas. "Peep, PEEP! Oh, good, I'm going for a day out at the seaside!"

Thomas was very pleased, and he chuffed along the track as fast as he could. He looked happy and cheerful again. "Let's hurry," he said to his Driver. "I can't wait to get back to the Shed to tell the others!"

**The Fat Controller took some photographs of Thomas
and his passengers just before they set off.**

These two pictures look the same, but there are 10 things that are different in this one. Can you find them?

ANSWERS

1.The tree in the background is missing. 2.The station window has gone. 3.Part of the platform roof has disappeared. 4.The little boy's spade is missing. 5.The lady in the blue dress has lost her hat. 6.Thomas' cabin window is missing. 7.The blonde lady now has a yellow dress on instead of red. 8.Thomas' coupling hook is missing. 9.Annie isn't behind Thomas anymore. 10.Thomas' number 1 has disappeared.

13

"That's the Way to Do It!"

1. All the engines came to see Thomas off, and the passengers waved from the coach windows.

2. He chuffed along his Branch Line to the little station near the beach.

3. The sun was shining, and Thomas had a rest in a siding beside the station. He had earned it!

4. Thomas watched the fun. The children built sandcastles and dug holes, and paddled in the sea.

5. The children had cold drinks, and Thomas did, too. His Driver made sure his big water tank was full.

6. It got very windy, and Thomas laughed when a gust of wind blew an ice cream out of its cone.

7. The wind blew his Driver's cap off and he had to run after it! "Faster, faster!" said Thomas.

8. As a special treat for the children, Bob, the Punch and Judy man, put up his little striped tent.

9. But an extra big gust of wind lifted the tent high into the air. "Peep, peep!" said Thomas.

10. The gust of wind blew the little tent far, far away. It went higher and higher up into the sky.

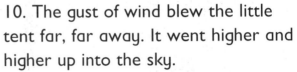

11. The wind dropped the tent a long way away, at the top of a tall tree. "Oh, no," said Bob.

12. "I can't do my show without the tent. The children will see me moving the puppets around. What a shame."

13. Bob was packing up his puppets when Thomas had an idea. "Use my cab instead of a tent," he said. "Stand inside the little doorway at the side."

14. "Yes!" said Bob. "The top part can be a little stage. Great idea, Thomas! Let's get everything ready!"

15. Soon the children were sitting on the ground in rows in the siding. Bob hid inside Thomas' cab.

16. The children laughed when the Punch and Judy puppets came out. Bob did funny voices for them.

17. Mister Punch had a long string of pretend sausages. He didn't want Toby the dog to eat them.

18. Mr Punch flung the sausages up into the air, and they landed – PLOP! – in Thomas' funnel! It wasn't meant to happen, but the children thought it was part of the show. They laughed and laughed.

19. "PEEP!" said Thomas, and he blew extra hard so that the sausages flew out of his funnel again.

20. The sausages ended up wrapped around Mr Punch's neck, like a big string of pink beads.

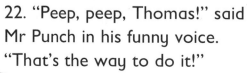

21. The children laughed even louder, and so did Thomas and his Driver and Fireman.

22. "Peep, peep, Thomas!" said Mr Punch in his funny voice. "That's the way to do it!"

Read this story yourself.
There are little pictures in place
of some of the words to help you.

 is a happy, helpful engine.

He likes to have fun with all

the ²  . He pulls them, then

he pushes them. He makes them

bump into each other.

James is very proud of his shiny

³  .

ANSWERS
1 Edward, 2 trucks, 3 red paint.

"I don't work with the dirty trucks," [4] told Edward.

"I do much more important work. I'm going to pull the [5] on the big express train."

When Edward heard James' [6] he looked up. What a surprise! James was pulling dirty old trucks filled with [7] .

He was covered in black [8]

ANSWERS 4 James, 5 carriages, 6 whistle, 7 coal, 8 dust.

The  were heavy, and

James got stuck going up the

. His  sent for help,

and Edward steamed up the line.

"Edward won't be able to help!"

said James.

The  blew his , and

waved his  .

Edward put his  on James

and pushed. It was hard work

and he made a lot of [16]  .

Puffs of [17] came out of his

[18] . Edward pushed James

to the top of the hill. He needed

a long drink of [19] when he

got there.

[20] said thank you. He had

learned a lesson. Edward's work

is not the same as his, but it is

just as important.

Percy is the little green tank engine who works in the Yard at the Big Station. He is engine number 6.

Percy loves playing tricks and jokes. One morning he stopped to say hello to Henry, the big green number 3 engine who pulls the train that carries the fish from the fishing boats at the harbour to the shops and markets on the mainland.

"You can stay in the Shed today, and have a rest," said Percy. "You've earned it. The Fat Controller wants me to pull the Flying Kipper."

"What?" said Henry, looking surprised. Then he smiled. "I don't believe you, Percy," he said. "This is another one of your little jokes. I'm going to pull the Flying Kipper, not you. Now off you go and try your tricks on someone else."

"If you say so," said Percy. "But don't blame me if you get into trouble for not doing what The Fat Controller tells you."

Cheeky Percy peeped and rushed off as fast as his wheels would go. He wanted Henry to think he really was going to collect the Flying Kipper from the harbour station.

Henry watched Percy as he chuffed off up the line. "I think he was joking," said poor Henry, "but I can't be sure."

Percy laughed as he rushed along. "I wonder if Henry will come after me?" he said.

Percy was enjoying his joke so much that he didn't take care. He got up more and more steam, and his little wheels turned faster and faster. Soon, Percy was going so fast that he couldn't stop!

A signalman watched Percy as he got closer to his signal box. He saw the danger, and changed the points just in time. Percy, still going at top speed, ran on to a long siding that was part of Thomas' Branch Line.

"HELP!" cried Percy. "I can't stop!"

Thomas heard Percy's call. He saw what was going to happen. "PEEP!" he said. "Smoke and cinders! Percy will run off the rails and crash if he doesn't stop soon."

But poor Percy couldn't stop.

Thomas knew that he had to help. He chuffed along the line until he saw Terence the Tractor, who was working in one of the fields.

Terence had once helped Thomas when he got into trouble, and the two of them became good friends. Terence doesn't need rails, and he can go anywhere on his special caterpillar tracks.

"PEEP!" said Thomas. "We need your help, Terence!"

"Coming!" called Terence, and he rumbled along on his big, wide tracks.

When Thomas told him about Percy, Terence knew just what to do.

He pushed some soft soil from the side of the siding. He made it into a big pile right at the end of the track.

He finished just in time, as runaway Percy rushed towards it. He still couldn't stop. When he saw the pile of soil he said, "Oh, no, I'm going to ... OOF!"

Percy crashed into the soil. It was a bit of a shock, but the soil was so soft that he wasn't hurt at all. He was covered in soil and bits of grass, and he was very hot and bothered, but he was safe and well.

He did feel a bit silly, and he had to say a big sorry to The Fat Controller – and to Henry, of course.

But do you think his adventure stopped cheeky Percy playing tricks and jokes on the other engines? No, of course it didn't!

The Branch Line Game

Thomas' Branch Line is a very busy one. He doesn't like being late, and he tries to get from one end of the track to the other as fast as he can.

Play this game on your own, or with a friend.
You need a die and a counter for each player.

Roll the die.
Move the number on the die.
If you score 2, move 2 places along the track, and so on.

If you land on

 have an extra throw

 go back 3

 go on 3

 go back 4

 go on 2

START | 1 | 2 | 3 | 4 | 5 | 6 | 7 | 8 | 9 | 10 | 11 | 12

30

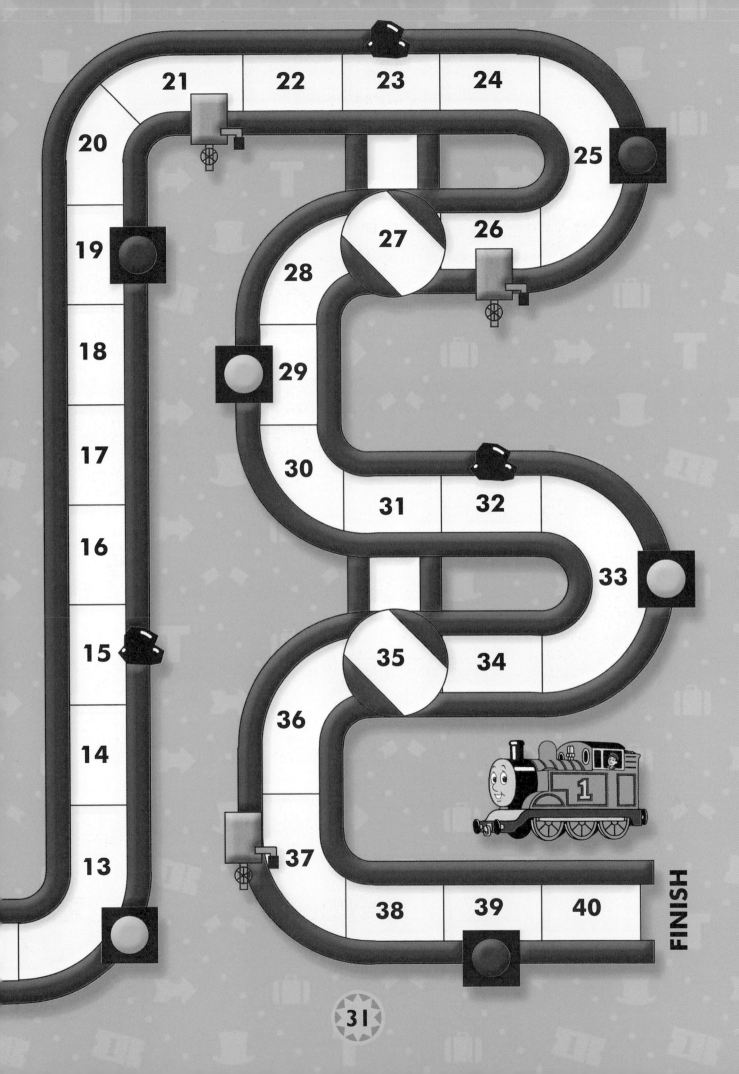

21 22 23 24

20

25

19

28 27 26

18

29

17

30

16

31 32

33

15

35 34

36

14

37

13

38 39 40

FINISH

Competition Time

22 PRIZES TO BE WON!

FIRST PRIZE

Thomas™ Pop Up Train
Complete with a spacious cabin and crawl through tunnel, it makes a fantastic play area for children. The Pop Up Train has detachable wheels and the Tunnel entrance has a tie-back cover for interconnectability.
The Thomas™ Pop Up Train can also be used both indoors and outside as this versatile product comes with rod and peg loops for extra stability in winds and carpet grippers for use indoors.

SECOND PRIZE

Thomas™ Pop Up Play Camp™.
The Play Camp displays Thomas The Tank Engine's unique design and the front door opening reveals Thomas' face which can be tied back for easy access. The Driver's Cab has a mesh window for ventilation and visibility and the rear tunnel entry has a tie-back flap for easy interconnectability. The Pop Up Play Camp also has the same features that make the product suitable for indoors and outdoors.

We also have 20 POP'n'FUN® Amazing Pocket Kites for our runners-up.

This large kite is ideal for beginners aged four and upwards. The kite features a brightly coloured picture of Thomas and the simple design allows it to be easily folded and taken anywhere.

HOW TO ENTER

All you have to do is unscramble these letters to spell out the name of a famous Thomas and Friends character:

RIS PATHOM THAT

Write your answer on a postcard or on the back of a sealed envelope (don't forget your name, address and age), and post it to:

THOMAS & FRIENDS ANNUAL COMPETITION, EGMONT WORLD, UNIT 7, MILLBANK HOUSE, RIVERSIDE PARK, BOLLIN WALK, WILMSLOW, CHESHIRE SK9 1BJ

POP 'n' FUN®
BY WORLDS APART®

RULES

1. 22 winners will be chosen at random and notified by post.
2. Judges' decision will be final. No correspondence will be entered into.
3. The winners' names will be made available from Egmont World (on request) after 5th February 2002. Please enclose a stamped addressed envelope for reply.
4. Employees (and their relatives) of Egmont World and their associated companies are not eligible to enter.
5. Entries are limited to one per person.
6. Competition is open to residents of the UK, Channel Islands, and Ireland only.
7. The Publishers reserve the right to vary prizes, subject to availability.
8. Closing date for entries is 26th January 2002.

The Really Useful Traction Engine

Some very important visitors were coming to the railway. A group of children from a school on the mainland had won a prize for their work on steam railways, and their special prize was a visit to meet Thomas and the other engines.

Sir Topham Hatt, The Fat Controller, spoke to the engines. "I want to make the visit extra special," he said. "What do you think the children will enjoy doing?"

The engines had some good ideas. "I'll take them for a ride on my Branch Line," said Thomas. "We can have a picnic by the river. Annie can carry the children and the picnic things can go in Clarabel."

"Splendid!" said The Fat Controller.

"I'll show the children some tricks with my trucks," said Percy. "They're sure to laugh when I stop them quickly and they all bump and bang into each other, like dodgem cars."

"Children like fast rides that spin them around, don't they?" said Gordon. "I'll give them a special ride on the turntable at the Big Station."

"Good idea," said Sir Topham. "It goes very fast if the men turn the handle quickly, like a fairground ride! They'll like that."

James is very proud of his shiny red paint. He doesn't usually like anyone to touch it. "The children could help the men to clean my paintwork and polish my funnel," he said. "Do you think they'll like that?"

"I'm sure they will," said Sir Topham. "Now, what can we do as an extra special treat just before the children go home?"

Edward thought hard. "Do you remember Trevor, the old traction engine?" he said. "I met him in the scrap yard near my station. He was going to be broken up because he was old fashioned. The Vicar rescued Trevor, and now he lives in the vicarage garden. I see him every day. His paint is spotless and his brass shines like gold. He saws wood, and does odd jobs, and takes the tractor's place if it breaks down. He loves children, and they love him. Let's ask him to give the children rides."

"What a good idea!" said The Fat Controller. "Please arrange it, Edward."

Trevor was very pleased to be asked to help. Edward and his Driver arranged for a long wooden seat to be bolted to Trevor's bunker so that he could carry a few children at once.

The children had a lovely day. They loved their ride on Thomas'
Branch Line. Sir Topham Hatt sent a surprise for the picnic – a big cake
made in the shape of an engine!

The ride on the big turntable made the children squeal with
laughter. But poor Gordon was quite glad when it was over. He had
whizzed around so fast that he felt very dizzy!

Percy made the children laugh, too, when he pushed and pulled
the trucks around, and they enjoyed polishing James' funnel until it
shone like gold.

Trevor the Traction Engine was happy to chuff around giving the
children rides until it was time for them to go home. Henry was going
to take them back to the harbour on the Flying Kipper.

The children said a big thank you to all the engines.

"I'm glad you had a good day," said Sir Topham. "What did you like best?"

The children all agreed that their rides on Trevor were the best bit of the day. "He's such a kind old traction engine," said one of the boys.

Sir Topham nodded his head. "I agree," he said.

Trevor was very pleased. "Some people say I'm old fashioned, but there's nothing wrong with that, is there?"

"No," said Edward. "Some people say I'm old fashioned, too, but I'm a Really Useful Engine, and so are you! Trevor, the Really Useful Traction Engine!"

Who am I?

The clues tell you about four of Thomas' friends.
Who are they?

1

I am a very fast engine.
My number is 3.
I am green.
I pull the Flying Kipper.
Who am I?

ANSWER:

_____

2

I am a tram engine.
My number is 7.
I have a coach called Henrietta.
My name begins with T.
Who am I?

ANSWER:

_____

3

I used to be called Montague.
I am green.
I have the letters G W R on
my side.
I work in the Yard with the trucks.
Who am I?

ANSWER:

_____

4

I am a twin engine.
I came to the railway from
Scotland.
My number is 9.
My twin is called Douglas.
Who am I?

ANSWER:

_____

Here are some of the engines to help you.
Can you find which ones are described on the
opposite page?

A Thomas Picture to Make

Have fun making this special Thomas picture.

You need:
- round paper plate
- piece of card
- safety scissors
- pencil
- ruler
- non-toxic glue
- cottonwool ball
- felt-tip pens or crayons

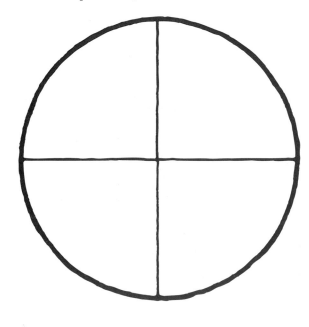

1. Ask a grown up to help you draw 2 lines to divide the plate into 4 pieces, like this:

2. Copy the outline of Thomas' face in pencil. Do it piece by piece.

3. Cut out a piece of card like this for Thomas' funnel, and glue it in place.

4. Colour your picture of Thomas.

5. Glue the cottonwool ball to the top of the funnel, like smoke.

Why not stick your Thomas picture on your bedroom door or wall, using a sticky tab?

Percy's Dream

Thomas loves working on his own little Branch Line. He's the only engine who works there, but he's never lonely. He always has someone to talk to. He chats to Annie and Clarabel, his coaches, as they steam along. He often meets his friend Bertie the Bus, and sees some of the other engines at the junction.

One day Thomas had been working hard, as usual. He hates being late, so he always goes as fast as he can. It sometimes means that he gets to the places he has to stop at too early.

This is just what happened when he was going to take some passengers to the junction to meet Bertie. He was early, so he had to wait for Bertie to arrive.

Thomas had a chat with little Percy, who had been working very hard in the Yard. He was feeling very tired, so he had stopped at the junction to get his steam back. He needed to rest for a while.

Percy yawned.

"It's lovely out here – YAWN – in the country, Thomas," said Percy. "You're very lucky – YAWN – to work out here, you know."

"I know I am," said Thomas.

"I wish I had my own line," said Percy, and he yawned again. "It would be a dream come true for me. How did you get – YAWN – your line?"

Thomas told him the story.

"My job was to take the coaches to the **Big Station** ready for the big engines to take out," said Thomas. "When they came back empty, I took them away again so the big engines could rest. I pushed and pulled trucks around the Yard, too."

"Just like – YAWN – me," said Percy.

"That's right," said Thomas. "But after a while I wasn't very happy just pulling trucks around. I wanted to see a bit of the world."

"Me – YAWN – too," said Percy.

"Anyway," said Thomas, "one day I saw James rushing along the line. The trucks were bossing him about, pushing him around – and they pushed him so hard that he went right off the line! I had an important job to do because I brought the breakdown train to help him. It has cranes for lifting engines that get into trouble."

"Good for – YAWN – you," said Percy.

"Oh, I made myself very useful that day," said Thomas. "I worked really hard. I pulled all the trucks that weren't broken out of the way. That was a struggle. Then when the men had repaired the line, the two cranes put poor James back on the line. But I still had more work to do, because it was my job to help James back to the Shed. He was in a bad way, and pushing a big engine like him along really tired me out. But I never complained, not once. I was happy to help."

"Just like a Really Useful – YAWN – Engine," said Percy.

"Peep!" said Thomas. "That's right. I had proved that I was a Really Useful Engine and The Fat Controller was very pleased with me. As a reward, he gave me my own Branch Line, and my own coaches, too, Annie and Clarabel."

Thomas had enjoyed telling Percy his story. "Who knows, Percy?" said Thomas. "If you work hard and make yourself Really Useful, perhaps The Fat Controller will give you your own Branch Line one day."

But Percy didn't reply. He was so tired that he had fallen fast asleep. "ZZZZZZZZZZZZZZZ..."
I wonder what Percy is dreaming about?

The Troublesome Trucks Game

Edward and Percy like working with the trucks. They can be troublesome, but Edward and Percy know how to handle them.

Play this game with a friend. One of you can play as Percy and the other as Edward.

Edward
START HERE

Edward

You need a die and 11 counters each. You can use buttons or coins if you like. Start from the Percy and Edward boxes. Take turns to roll the die. If you score 4, move 4 places along the railway track, and so on. Going under the track counts as one space. When you land on a truck, cover one of the trucks in your Yard with a counter or button. Keep going around the track until one of you covers all your trucks to win the game.

Percy
START HERE

Percy

49

1. Harold the Helicopter works at the airfield near the harbour. He whizzes around all day.

2. Harold is proud that he's such a modern machine. He teased old engines like Percy and Thomas.

3. "You're old fashioned compared to me," he said. "I'm like a whirly bird, I can go up and down, and I can hover."

4. "I don't have to get around on rails, like you railway engines," he said. "I can fly anywhere I like."

5. "I'm fast, too!" said Harold. "Look!" Thomas and Percy chuffed off. "Take no notice of him," said Thomas.

6. One day there was an urgent message at the Big Station. Henry had come off the rails!

7. "This is an emergency," said The Fat Controller. "Henry has to be moved as quickly as possible."

8. "He's carrying lots of passengers, and some of them may be hurt. We need to get to him."

9. Harold had just dropped off a visitor, and he said he would help. "I'm fast, and I can fly anywhere."

10. The Fat Controller sent Harold to help Henry, but he sent Thomas, too, with the breakdown train.

11. "I know you are much slower, Thomas," he said. "But that can't be helped. Do your best."

12. Thomas wished he could go faster. "Harold will have done everything before I even get there," he said.

13. But Thomas got a surprise! When he went round a bend in the line he saw Harold sitting in a field.

14. "You WERE fast, Harold!" said Thomas. "Have you rescued Henry already?"

15. Harold didn't look as pleased with himself as he usually did. "I can't help," he said. "Sorry."

16. "Henry came off the rails in the tunnel. I can't fly in there, because my arms are too long."

17. The tunnel was no problem for Thomas, of course, and he took the breakdown train to Henry.

18. Henry was soon back on the rails. He was a bit shaken up, but there was no damage.

19. "I haven't been much use, have I?" Harold asked. "Is there anything I can do to help?"

20. "I'm sure there must be one job you can do," said Thomas. "Now let me think …"

21. "There is something," said Thomas. "You can take a message back to the Big Station."

22. "People use birds called pigeons to carry messages," said cheeky Thomas.

23. "You said you can fly just like a whirly bird, Harold, so you can do the same job. Please tell The Fat Controller that Henry is fine," said Thomas. "And that I'm in charge! Peep, peep!"

Count with Thomas

Find these things in the big picture and count them.
Write the numbers in the boxes.

57

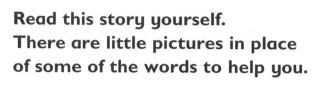
Read this story yourself.
There are little pictures in place
of some of the words to help you.

Gordon is a very proud engine.

He thinks his job pulling the

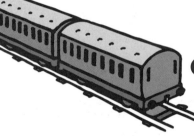 of the express train is

very important. "Not like your

job, ²  ," he says, "pulling

and pushing those messy ³

around the Yard all day."

ANSWERS   1 carriages, 2 Percy, 3 trucks

Percy is a cheeky engine who

likes playing tricks.

One morning he tells  ⁴

that he has a message from

 ⁵. Someone important is

coming to present a ⁶  at the

big show. He wants Gordon to

take her from ⁷ .

"But you have to look special," says Percy. "You have to be covered in ⁸ ." Percy's  ⁹ and fireman cover Gordon in flowers. They put ropes of ¹⁰  on his sides. They put ¹¹  and ¹² flowers on his ¹³ . Gordon even has a bunch of sunflowers stuck in his ¹⁴ !

When Gordon steams into the

Big Station, all his friends laugh

at him. It was a trick!

Gordon is very angry. POOP!

He blows big clouds of ¹⁵

out of his funnel and all the

¹⁶  fly into the air.

"That will teach you not to make

fun of me!" says Percy.

ANSWERS 15 steam, 16 sunflowers

THOMAS
& FRIENDS

1